DATE DUE

FEB 2 2 2003	
APR - 9 2004	
JUL 5 2004	
JUL 5 2005	
AUG 1 5 2005	
AUG 2 5 2005	
JAN 1 8 2006	

Put Beginning Readers on the Right Track with ALL ABOARD READING™

The All Aboard Reading series is especially for beginning readers. Written by noted authors and illustrated in full color, these are books that children really and truly *want* to read—books to excite their imagination, tickle their funny bone, expand their interests, and support their feelings. With five different reading levels, All Aboard Reading lets you choose which books are most appropriate for your children and their growing abilities.

Picture Readers—for Ages 3 to 6
Picture Readers have super-simple texts, with many nouns appearing as rebus pictures. At the end of each book are 24 flash cards—on one side is the rebus picture; on the other side is the written-out word.

Pre-Level 1—for Ages 4 to 6
First Friends, First Readers have a super-simple text starring lovable recurring characters. Each book features two easy stories that will hold the attention of even the youngest reader while promoting an early sense of accomplishment.

Level 1—for Preschool through First-Grade Children
Level 1 books have very few lines per page, very large type, easy words, lots of repetition, and pictures with visual "cues" to help children figure out the words on the page.

Level 2—for First-Grade to Third-Grade Children
Level 2 books are printed in slightly smaller type than Level 1 books. The stories are more complex, but there is still lots of repetition in the text, and many pictures. The sentences are quite simple and are broken up into short lines to make reading easier.

Level 3—for Second-Grade through Third-Grade Children
Level 3 books have considerably longer texts, harder words, and more complicated sentences.

All Aboard for happy reading!

For Alison, with
heart and sole—S.H.

For everyone who tries and tries:
don't give up! You can do it!—A.W.

Text copyright © 2002 by Susan Hood. Illustrations copyright © 2002 by Amy Wummer.
All rights reserved. Published by Grosset & Dunlap, a division of Penguin Putnam Books
for Young Readers, 345 Hudson Street, New York, NY 10014. GROSSET & DUNLAP and
ALL ABOARD READING are trademarks of Penguin Putnam Inc. Published simultaneously in
Canada. Printed in the USA.

Library of Congress Cataloging-in-Publication Data is available.

ISBN 0-448-42835-0 (GB)   A B C D E F G H I J
ISBN 0-448-42676-5 (pbk)   A B C D E F G H I J

ALL
ABOARD
READING™

Level 1
Preschool-Grade 1

LOOK!
I Can Tie My Shoes!

By Susan Hood
Illustrated by Amy Wummer

Grosset & Dunlap • New York

I love shoes!

I love high-tops.

I love flip-flops.

I love jellies.

I love wellies!

Shoes with bows
or cutout toes.

Funny flippers . . .

and bunny slippers!

Yes, I love shoes!

Sale

But not these shoes!

Mom asks me why.

"I cannot tie . . ."

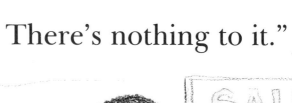

"You can do it.
There's nothing to it."

Mom says,

"I'll show you how.

Right here, right now."

Tie a loop.

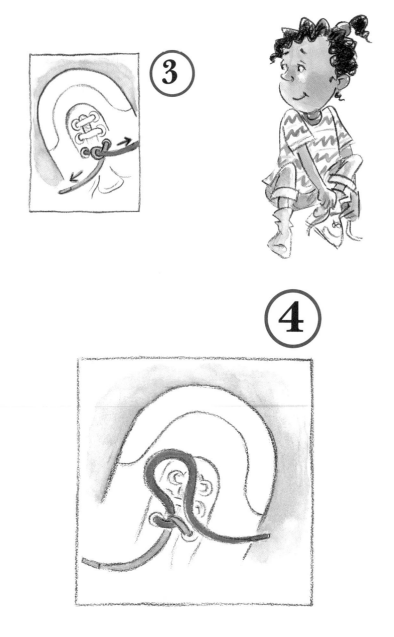

Then wrap like this.

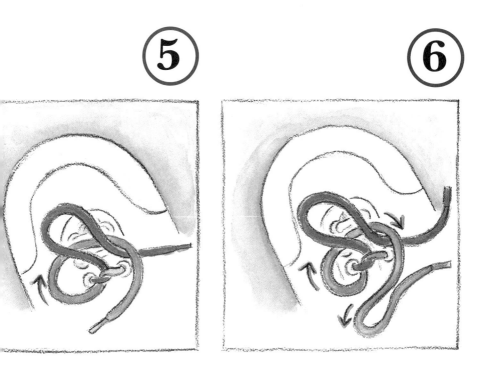

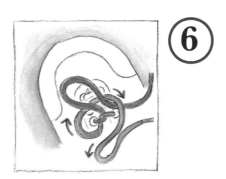

⑥

Go under.

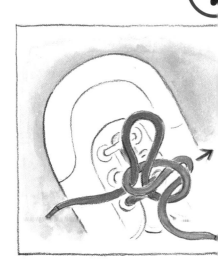

⑦

⑧

Pull.

Oops! I missed!

I try and try
to learn to tie!

Loop a loop.

Wrap like this.

Go under.

Pull.

Hug and kiss!

I can do it!

Nothing to it!